HUNT FOR THE BLACK CORAL

ADVENTURE 2

TREASURE, SUSPENSE, PIRATES, and the DEVIL'S TRIANGLE

GREG BIBA

Hunt for the Black Coral is a work of fiction.
The well-known people, events, and places that figure into
the story are products of the author's imagination or are
used fictitiously. Any resemblance to actual events, locales,
or persons, living or dead, is coincidental.

Inspiration and Editing by the Waupaca Writers Club
and the Waupaca Area Public Librarians
Editing: Richard Sweitzer, Dawn Biba, Adam Biba,
Kaylee Biba, Bill Riemer, Sarah Hanneman, Lori Jungers,
Kerry Leuders, Shirley Ellis

Student Editor: Logan Rogney

Proofreading and Editing: Molly Eaton

Cover Art: Tricia Price

Illustrations: Shirley Ellis

ISBN - 9798653195020

another
fine
print
by

Design
Fineprintgraphix@gmail.com

The lure of searching for shipwreck treasure, including the rare black coral, has taken a family of scuba divers, Greg, Dawn, Adam, and Kaylee, far into the mysterious Bermuda Triangle.

For centuries, what went into the Bermuda Triangle has not always come out. There are countless stories that have never been explained of events above the surface and below.

In *Hunt for the Black Coral* the greed of the Captain and First Mate leads to dangerous, life-threatening situations.

Will the family's dive adventure break their spirit, or will they succeed to go on another adventure?

Chapter 1

HUNT FOR THE BLACK CORAL

In Greg's latest adventure magazine, there was an advertisement from a salvage company that was looking for certified scuba divers. If hired, these divers were to search for treasure from sunken ships off the southern coast of Florida.

Greg told Dawn, Adam, and Kaylee, "I know that we are fresh off *A Stratton Lake Mystery,* where we luckily found the last of Al Capone's bank heist treasure. Since we are all certified scuba divers, what about using the last portion of the money to go on a new treasure hunt?" He added, "The adventure magazine advertisement says that we would embark on an ocean adventure and be taught how to search for and salvage rare, valuable sunken artifacts."

"Count us in! When can we go?" Adam and Kaylee shouted.

"Here we go again, another adventure," Dawn said with a grin.

It was just a few years since their son, Adam, and daughter, Kaylee, had become certified.

The family recently went on a diving adventure and discovered a shipwreck in the cold, October waters of Lake Superior, off the coast of Northern Wisconsin.

This shipwreck dive was a marvelous experience for the family, but it would be nothing compared to the next dive adventure, which would take them into the *Bermuda Triangle.*

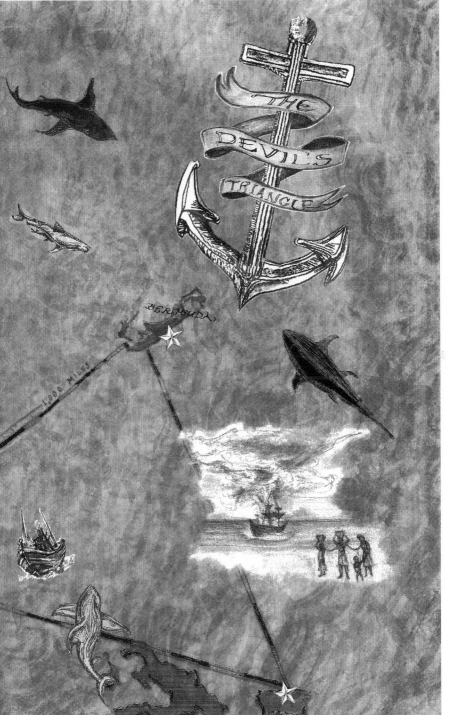

Chapter 2

PREPARATION

Dawn had been a certified scuba dive instructor in Florida and had taken numerous trips to the area before. She told Greg, Adam and Kaylee about the incredible waterspouts, sharks, stingrays, octopuses, dolphins, crabs and starfish. Her vivid memories made the possibility of finding sunken treasure more exciting.

Adam asked, "Is it true that nurse sharks are man-eaters?"

Dawn shook her head and said, "They are not very dangerous as long as you leave them alone. The nurse sharks are gray-brown in color and have jaws to crush and eat shellfish and even coral, but prefer to dine on fish, shrimp, and squid."

Kaylee, also curious, asked, "Are the awesome waterspouts people see over the ocean different from the tornadoes we see on land?"

"I saw only fair weather waterspouts. Usually they are relatively small, typically a few hundred feet across or less with average wind speeds of near 50 miles per hour. They only last a few minutes. The waterspouts can develop underneath tall cumulus clouds."

Greg thought to ask Dawn, "What about those vicious looking barracudas you've seen?"

"The barracudas can range from 4-6 feet in length. They reside near the top of the water and near coral reefs and sea grasses. Like sharks, some species of barracuda are reputed to be dangerous to swimmers."

"Why would the barracudas be dangerous to swimmers?" Greg questioned.

"They are scavengers, and may mistake snorkelers for large predators, following them in hopes of eating the remains of their prey." Dawn added, "We always left them alone, giving them the proper respect they deserve and they left us alone."

The gathering place for important family decisions was the Biba kitchen. Greg loved the view through the large picture window of the rose and vegetable garden that Dawn painstakingly tended. While in the kitchen and enjoying a breakfast of pancakes and eggs, Dawn said confidently to Greg, Adam, and Kaylee, "Packing should be easy for us because we can rent our gear at the dive location."

"The timing of the diving adventure is perfect because it's the same as our summer vacations from teaching. The timing is perfect for Adam and Kaylee also because they will be on their break from college. Now that they are both young adults, the legal age of 15 for Open Water Dive Certification in Florida is no longer an issue," Dawn added.

"Why don't you take your sketchbook Kaylee?" Adam urged, "We all admire your chalk drawings of our family vacations."

Dawn continued to tell Adam and Kaylee, "Since most of the time will be on a boat or in the water, we only need to bring the essentials of swimsuits, suntan lotion, bathroom supplies, and a couple changes of clothes. Dad and I will bring our laptops and pack them in our carry-on luggage."

"Who will take care of our mischievous cats while we're gone?" Adam asked. "I also wonder if the Captain or anyone on board our boat might have a guitar," he added while smiling.

"I've already asked Uncle Pat," Dawn replied. "He will also take care of watering the plants, picking up the mail, and mowing the grass. Being able to pay for the flight to Florida, the cost of the dive trip, and miscellaneous expenses isn't an issue. We've saved the money from our discovery of Al Capone's bank heist money around Stratton Lake. We've also been able to cover the cost of this dive adventure from my teaching part time as a driver's education instructor."

Greg was at home in Waupaca, standing in the doorway of his office, where all of the family's scuba dive equipment was stored, when he reached Mr. Steven Schultz, from the Acme Maritime Salvage Company in Fort Lauderdale, Florida.

"What are the typical lengths of your dive and salvage trips Steven?"

"Usually, divers will contract for either one or two months at a time. If we're lucky to find anything of value, the crews stay at sea for about a week. Then they haul their finds into port, provision the boat, and head back out."

Greg asked Captain Steven for a short period of time to talk to his family about the specifics of their conversation. Mr. Schultz would get a call back right away with a possible dive commitment.

Greg and Dawn researched the Captain of the Acme Maritime Salvage Company and learned that he was a certified Dive Master. He held the Exploration and Recovery Permits as administered by Chapter 1A-31, Florida Administrative Code, which legally allowed archaeological excavation.

After careful consideration of everything that had to be taken care of before their departure, a one month commitment was made with Captain Steven Schultz. Upon arrival diving and salvage work would begin immediately.

DANIA BEACH

The Antique Capital of the South

POPULATION 29,000

Summer vacations are short, so Dawn arranged a direct flight for four from Chicago to Fort Lauderdale, Florida for the following week.

Adam asked his Mom, "What are the duties of the Dive Master?"

"Duties include planning all the dives, what depths the dives will reach, and how long each person should remain at those depths. If anyone stays down too long, the Dive Master determines the wait before diving again. He also provides snacks and lunch."

Chapter 3

"WE'LL ALL BE RICH!"

Not long after arriving in Florida to the Fort Lauderdale/Hollywood International Airport, Greg rented a car and drove his family south. From the plane to the sun and warm sands of Dania Beach, the drive was about three miles.

"This looks like a great place for a future vacation," Kaylee said. "I see awesome looking ice cream parlors. Dad, I noticed a big Casino right on the beach that you and Mom might have fun."

"That sign on the side of the road says Dania Beach is 'The Antique Capital of the South—population 29,000'." Dawn replied.

The converted boathouse looked ancient even for this older part of the city. It used to be an office when the lobster industry in the area was booming. Greg wasn't worried though, he knew these guys lived for the open water and these old docks were just temporary lodging between forays into the big blue.

Rather than being nervous or scared about diving in the ocean, the Bibas were very excited about discussing the upcoming dive and salvage goals with Steven.

Captain Schultz told his new dive family, "I have recently heard of other so called Dive and Salvage Companies that have worked near, but not in the *Bermuda Triangle.* They have discovered small amounts of gold doubloons and silver bars." Steven continued, "My team and I are the best at finding the most valuable treasures known, and feel that if we sail into the *Triangle,* we may be able to find the mother-load. We have found more gold and silver treasure than larger salvage companies over the years."

Greg and Dawn were curious and asked Steven, "So, you feel that diving in the *Triangle* will reward us with a lot of treasure? Is this why your salvage company is not diving

in our agreed southern Florida coast location, and is it legal to sail into the Bermuda Triangle?"

Greg continued, "Have you studied the archives for vessels lost at sea which contained any gold or silver?"

"Yes, I have studied shipwrecks, and it is legal for even pleasure crafts to sail into the *Triangle*. The famous African slave ship, *San Miguel,* was known to have sailed into the Bermuda Triangle, and this haul could be one of the most valuable discoveries ever."

They were told that the *San Miguel* sank over 300 years ago in the *Triangle*, as it made its way from Africa to Cuba, then on to Jamestown, Virginia, the city where slaves had been sold at auction from 1619-1864.

Greg asked Steven, "If *San Miguel* was indeed a slave ship, why would it have valuable treasures on board to excavate?"

"Ships transporting slaves from the years 1619-1864, were required by maritime law to hoist flags, colored red and white. The biggest slave port was out of Luanda, Angola. This is where the Captain must have a manifest, which would include a description of cargo and what was declared before they set sail. It was well known pirates would frequent these coastal waters and would bypass slave ships, because the vessels were not carrying any precious stones, gold doubloons, pieces of eight, copper, silver bars, or the most rare and valuable of African jewelry: *black coral.*" He continued, "It was rumored the captain of the slave ship, *San Miguel,* knew it could carry valuables without being bothered by pirates because it illegally flew the red and white colors even though there were no slaves aboard."

Luis added, "There were times when the ship's manifest would have to be faked prior to leaving Africa. After secretly loading gold doubloons, pieces of eight, copper, silver bars, and black coral, only sugar and rum would be left visible to port authorities."

Greg asked, "Where did the treasures come from?"

"There were ancient and dangerous gold mines found in Ghana, and along the rivers of Volta and Ankobra."

"Were there any other valuables from Africa that may have been traded with other countries?"

"Yes, gold was traded for salt and slaves with the Berber tribes of Northern Africa. The Berbers used gold and salt for currency and traded with the Arab world, of the Middle East." Steven added, "Between the 10th and 13th centuries the South African Kingdom of Mapungubwe thrived due to their natural resources like gold located in what is now modern day Zimbabwe but formerly known as Rhodesia. By the 1300s, trading in gold had begun. Gold was mined in Zimbabwe and transported to the port city of Kilwa Kisiwani in exchange for pottery, porcelain, and silk from China and Persia."

Dawn wondered, "What is the possibility of the ship going down as a result of a hurricane?"

Steven told his treasure hunters, "Hurricanes off the southern coast of Florida are common during the summer months and the captain of the doomed *San Miguel* decided to sail north towards the *Bermuda Triangle* to avoid any severe storms."

Greg asked, "If the captain avoided the hurricanes by sailing north, what caused the *San Miguel* to sink?"

"There had been rumors of modern ships losing their compass headings upon entering the *Triangle*, as well as ships that date back to the times of Christopher Columbus. This is one of the two places on earth that a magnetic compass does point towards the true north. Normally it points toward the magnetic north. The difference between the two is known as compass variation. The amount of variation changes by as much as 20 degrees as one circumnavigates the earth. If this compass variation or error is not compensated for, a navigator could find himself far off course and in deep trouble." The Captain smiled and added, "This can be a very misleading statement. Before a navigator could even chart a course he would have to know the amount of variation and the fact that magnetic north is not at the North Pole. The magnetic north of this planet is at Prince of Wales Island in the Northwest Territory of Canada." This made Greg raise an eyebrow.

He hadn't brought his family all this way for a failed seaman's folly. This was supposed to be a family adventure to find a few trinkets in the sand, not a life-or-death journey into the *Bermuda Triangle*.

"Just follow my orders," Steven added confidently, "And we'll all be rich!"

Chapter 4

FINDING BLACK CORAL

Steven's discussion about intentionally sailing north into the Bermuda Triangle to avoid a summertime hurricane made Greg and Dawn start to feel somewhat skeptical about their captain and their safety on this treasure hunt.

Adam and Kaylee needed to know more about what they were diving for. "What kind of valuable treasures are we talking about here?" Adam asked getting excited.

"Gold doubloons, silver bars, and hopefully the rare *black coral*" the Captain answered.

"What makes the black coral so rare?" Kaylee asked.

"Before slaves were captured and brought to the United States, some of the men of the tribes were deep-sea divers and were able to dive deep enough to bring up coral that was able to be fashioned into necklaces and be used for trade with other tribes. These native divers would plunge more than 100 feet beneath the surface of the ocean without air tanks. Only occasionally would the bravest men dive much deeper and bring up the rare black coral." He added, "Because it was so hard to get black coral was very valuable and thought to bring good luck to whomever possessed it. The coral was considered to be precious and was used in the oldest form of gemstone jewelry with pieces dating back to the time of the woolly mammoth. When polished, this rare coral shines with such luster you can almost see your own reflection in it." Captain Steven explained.

"I've seen this black coral, " Dawn chimed in. "It's a stunning contrast against gold and makes a wonderful gift. When jewelry is made, purchasers get a sticker with their purchase which certifies that the coral is original, legally harvested, and that it is authentic. It even predates the use of another ancient favorite from the sea, *pearls!* Each coral gemstone color has its own distinct quality. Black coral is exotic and I've heard it's long been considered to guard against misfortune."

The Captain continued, "Coral is on the endangered species list. However, I have a license to harvest, but only those pieces that have broken off naturally," he said, waving his finger at the crew. "Never cut or break any living coral off the reef!"

Hearing what treasures await them, the Biba family were convinced to go into the *Bermuda Triangle.*

Chapter 5

SETTING SAIL

Bright and early the next day they left the gorgeous beaches and warm waves, setting sail towards the *Bermuda Triangle*. After leaving the busy port, Luis told everyone the many cruise ships out on the horizon were heading for the Caribbean and Mexico everyday.

Even though Steven tried to be convincing about being able to make it into the *Triangle* with no problems, he seemed overconfident, so it made our anxious couple a little edgy about the area they were taking their kids into. They felt this expedition was not going to be just routine.

The Captain told everyone that at a cruise of 20 knots at sea or about 23 miles per hour, and a distance of roughly 500 miles, it would take 25-30 hours to reach the center of the *Bermuda Triangle,* where he thought it would be their best chance of finding their treasure.

While near the port, and having a wi-fi connection, Greg and Dawn found plenty of time to do some research on their laptops where they found additional theories explaining why so many other ships disappeared. Some explanations were electronic fog, tropical cyclones, methane gas, and the souls of the African slaves.

Meanwhile, while they were occupied with their *Bermuda Triangle* research. Adam and Kaylee, at the urging of Luis, who was the first mate, cook, and life long friend to Captain Steven, were refreshing their dive skills. This meant reviewing their logs, basic safety skills, including buddy breathing, and looking over Mom and Dad's dive equipment as well as their own.

"Nice job *learning the ropes,*" Luis commented.

"What does that mean?" Kaylee asked.

"Oh, sorry, that means you have reviewed and understand how to do things better as we get ready for our salvage mission. You'll have to get used to my nautical phrases and expressions. I guess I have been at sea for so long that these sayings have been incorporated into my everyday language."

Greg told Dawn, "The souls of the African slaves is one of the most significant theories of why slave ships were never seen again. The *Triangle* comprises souls of slaves who had been thrown overboard by sea captains on their journey to the States. In his book *Healing the Haunted*, British psychiatrist Dr. Kenneth McAll claimed "a continuous haunted sound (like mournful singing) could be heard while sailing in the *Bermuda Triangle* waters."

Dawn added, "In my research, the *Bermuda Triangle* covers an area of 440,000 square sea miles, or nearly the size of Alaska. I don't think we should be worried after all about going into the *Triangle* because it is one of the most heavily traveled shipping lanes in the world with ships frequently crossing through to get to ports in America, Europe, and the Caribbean. Also, the Captain does not think going into *sacred waters* is an issue."

Dawn asked Luis, "Did the trade winds benefit any of the early explorers coming near the *Triangle*?"

"Historically the routes were also shaped by the powerful influence of winds and currents. From the main trading nations of Western Europe, it was much easier to sail westward after first going south and reaching the trade winds; thus arriving in the Caribbean rather than going straight west to the North American mainland." Luis concluded, "Returning from North America, it was easiest to follow the Gulf Stream in a northeasterly direction using the westerlies."

While the inquisitive couple were doing their research, Adam and Kaylee, being mischievous, and other than doing some deep sea fishing with Luis, did occupy themselves occasionally by sneaking over to dip their tin cups into the Captain's rum punch, which was in a barrel near his cabin door. Kaylee also pulled out her sketchbook from the safety of a waterproof bag.

Greg yawned, "Where's the day gone?" They looked out onto the horizon at some humpback whales surfacing gently. "Bermuda protects the humpbacks in this area; they are threatened by ship strikes, fishing nets, also by pollution and ocean noise," he added.

Kaylee had a great time sketching the rarely seen humpbacks before they followed a school of small fish and plankton below the surface.

"You and Greg should get some sleep Dawn," Steven said, "We have about an hour of sailing in the morning before we start diving tomorrow."

Their cabins were small with only bunk beds and little room to sit up. "Now I know what your dad's cocoon-like sleeping arrangements were when he was in the US Navy in World War II," Greg said laughing.

Because all of the cabins were now being used, and the fact that storms did spring up often late at night, instead of sleeping in a hammock on deck, Luis shared the Captain's cabin, located near the engine room and the stern of the boat. Rather than using bunk beds, they both slept on larger individual cots. There was just enough room to share a toilet and shower. There was also a table to play cards. Instead of playing cards the rest of the night, the Captain and Luis shared their late night bottle of rum punch.

"Remember Luis you have first watch tonight when we finish our rum punch," the Captain said without a smile.

"What's wrong Steven?" Luis asked.

"You know as well as I," he slurred, as he pointed to the ten year old newspaper articles that were plastered all over their cabin, including pictures of Steven's father.

Luis knew just how obsessed the Captain was when he would find the newspaper articles that he had thrown in the trash, ending back up on the walls of the Captain's quarters. The article was entitled, "Search Efforts Futile For Captain Aquarius Christopher, After Once In A Lifetime Hurricane!"

"You haven't talked about that night you lost your father on a dive in almost ten years" Luis replied. "You need to get it off your chest or you'll put our new friends on this dive trip in danger."

"We need to honor my father's memory by having a successful treasure hunt."

Luis reminded Steven, "When you drink too much the night before a big dive, you don't think clearly. You do not want to be *three sheets to the wind* or be someone that is very, very drunk."

"All right, I'll talk about it, but we'll have to get the dive tanks, fins, wet suits and masks out on deck before it gets light in a few hours. Please go and wake up our guests when the sun shows itself on the horizon. We can meet up on deck after making a pot of coffee, so I can try to make them understand what has happened."

At sunrise the blurry eyed family joined Captain Steven, who was already sipping a mug of strong, black coffee. He was sitting near the dive gear that would need to be set up properly for the upcoming dives of the day. Upon being woken up at sunrise, Greg wasn't too happy about hitting his head on the entrance of his cabin after only getting to sleep for a short time.

As Greg and Dawn sat on a couple of old barrels, Kaylee and Adam tried to make themselves comfortable, while sitting down on the smooth, wet deck. Luis was pacing behind the Captain worrying what he would say to calm everyone's ruffled feathers.

"The reason Luis was on board was because he and his family decided to escape from the poverty of Havana, Cuba and float to Florida on a life-raft. Coincidentally, he is the same age as I am," explained the Captain. "Their raft was almost sunk by a severe storm. My father and I happened to be in the area and gave Luis and his family a hand and work aboard our salvage company boat."

After slurping down a big sip of his strong coffee, Steven stated, "When I was young, about sixteen years old, my father and I started our salvage company."

Luis always appreciated Steven and his father for not telling the immigration authorities about his family's escape from Cuba. Some people were lucky enough to make it to the shores of the U.S. and were granted political asylum. Since Luis and his family were saved by the Captain and his father, and given steady work on board the salvage boat, they had felt obligated to stay with Steven.

When my father was preparing to dive for sunken treasure in the same area that we are in now, we encountered hurricane-like weather. He was thrown overboard, not to be seen again."

After a moment of silence, Steven composed himself and with a lump in his throat concluded, "The reason I picked the name *ACME* for our salvage boat was to honor my father's legacy. The first two letters, "AC," stand for his name, Aquarius Christopher. Aquarius means "water bearer," in Latin. Christopher was known as the patron saint of travelers and controversial discoverer of the new world."

Luis interrupted, trying to lighten the mood. With a smile he said, "Captain, we'll have to repaint our boat soon. Over the years, the sea salt has worn away half of the Acme Maritime Salvage Company name. Since *AC* are the only letters remaining from *ACME*, we can rename her again as the *AQUARIUS CHRISTOPHER* to honor your father."

Everyone appreciated the Captain's honesty about the tragic loss of his father many years ago. It made everyone aware of why searching for treasure in this same area was important and might make him distracted. This was coincidentally the same location as the ill fated sinking of the San Miguel slave ship that held so much treasure.

No sooner than Luis and the Captain arranged the dive equipment on deck for his Acme Maritime Salvage Company, the sun began to rise, which meant it was time for Luis to start breakfast for everyone.

Steven wasn't himself after sharing the real reason for traveling to the *Bermuda Triangle,* and Luis was becoming more concerned about his best friend's emotional well being than the safety of everyone on their dive.

SEARCH EFFORTS FUTILE FOR

CAPTAIN AQUARIUS CHRISTOPHER,

AFTER ONCE IN A LIFETIME

HURRICANE!

Chapter 6

DROP ANCHOR

Possibly the most talked about paranormal region, the Bermuda Triangle was also known as the *Devil's Triangle*. Although holding its natural beauty, it was an area so vast that being on board a little boat made one feel all alone in the universe, especially when there was nothing but you and water.

After the upfront discussion given by Captain Schultz, Adam and Kaylee saw a waterspout off in the distance and the most beautiful rainbow they had ever seen. It stretched across the sky from one end of the horizon to the other. These rainbows were typically visible after a short, but not severe thunderstorm.

"I'm glad that you're sketching that rainbow Kaylee. You sure don't see those back in Waupaca. There's way too many trees." Adam commented.

It didn't take too long for all on board to start smelling the cook's extraordinary signature dish; scrambled eggs and lobster.

Out on deck Adam pointed out dolphins, "Check out the dolphins! They're keeping up with us, swimming and jumping."

They continued to sail towards the *Triangle*. The waves were getting choppier as Steven called down to the engine room for more speed.

"Yes, Captain, I'll give it all I can!" Luis shouted from down below, over the sound of the two large diesel engines.

After an hour of what felt like the roughest boat ride in history, Greg and Dawn were relieved when the Captain finally called to the engine room, "Stop all engines, drop anchor."

The boat was still rocking back and forth as the first mate rang the ship's bell and called, *"All hands on deck!* Everyone needs to help."

Chapter 7

THE BERMUDA TRIANGLE, UNEXPLAINED

Steven checked his depth finder and maps and exclaimed, "We're now inside of the *Bermuda Triangle,* where another salvage company recently found some gold doubloons and silver bars."

"Everything is *hunky-dory,* Captain, " Luis chimed in, "Our location is perfect."

Greg asked, "Why aren't the other salvage companies looking anymore?"

Luis replied, "My guess is the salvage company found the treasure which drifted here from deeper within the *Triangle* and when they couldn't find any more, they were either afraid to go in further, or the only way they could find valuables was to search the seabed by hand."

Steven hid the fact that pirates had been seen frequenting these waters, and could be a distinct possibility of why salvage divers did not stay too long in this area.

Dawn asked, "Why do you think a salvage team would be afraid to search farther into the *Bermuda Triangle* when they were so close to getting more treasure?"

"There are many unexplained reasons why ships or planes enter the *Triangle* and don't come out. The captain of the other salvage company may have personally known others that thought they could find treasure, entered, and were not seen or heard from again."

To calm his seafaring client's nerves about unexplained rumors of missing persons, Steven thought he'd better get the salvage work started just inside the *Triangle.* With luck, finding enough treasure would keep everyone excited and willing to continue on.

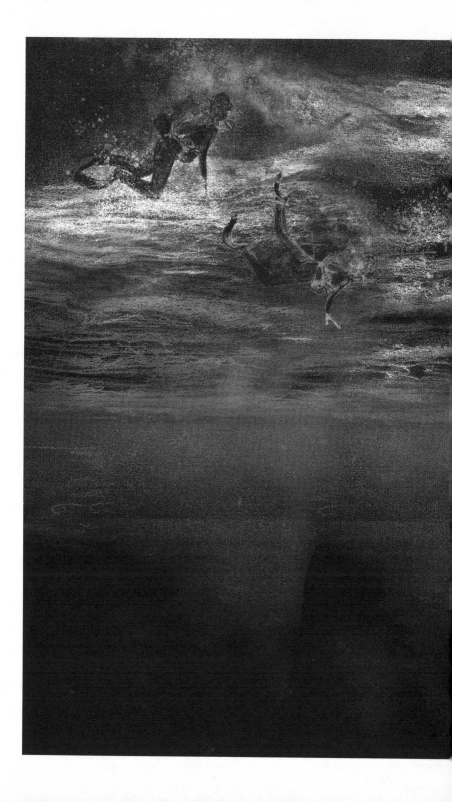

Chapter 8

BUDDY BREATHING

"Drop the dive ladder and the anchor line!" ordered the Captain.

"Captain Schultz runs a tight ship!" Luis yelled, so all on deck could hear. "He is extremely strict on how we should stay organized."

The dive depth of 130 feet, or the distance of a 43 yard field goal in football, an anchor line was necessary to hang onto in order to guide descent.

Everyone held on tight as the boat bounced up and down in the surge. The whole family put on their dive suits and followed the first mate, Luis to the bow.

"Ready?" Luis asked, "On the count of three you jump."

Before he could get to three, Adam and Kaylee had already put on their masks, gloves and fanny packs, ready to discover treasure. They had already plunged into the murky water--trying to descend about 130 feet to the bottom, where the gold, silver, and black coral were promised by Steven.

Even though they were nervous, they grabbed the anchor line and started to make their way hand over hand towards the treasures below. Adam and Kaylee were more excited, than anxious about the deep dive.

Suddenly, Adam felt something bump up against his leg, but could not see what it was because of the murkiness of the warm water. He remembered Luis talking about giant squid being in the area. He also mentioned Sperm whales were the only natural predators of the squid.

"Let's catch up to them, Dawn," Greg exclaimed.

Knowing the kids were confident divers, they did not worry about their head-start towards the bottom. The visibility of the water cleared as they made their way deeper.

Greg and Dawn were floating on the top of the water, as the waves were slamming into their masks with forceful authority. While they waited for the water to clear so they could see below the surface, Greg noticed that something was not right. He motioned to Dawn to look down, and they saw their young scuba divers were not searching for treasure, but rather heading back up to the surface, swimming close to each other.

Anxiously, Greg and Dawn waited for Adam and Kaylee to swim their way to the surface. The current of the water grew increasingly more choppy towards the surface as they slowly made their way to safety. If they had been able to make the dive deeper, Adam and Kaylee would have noticed the calmness of the seabed below.

They all grabbed the side of the boat, and with the help of Luis, slid into the bottom of the boat, lifting off their masks and gear. Adam and Kaylee gasped for air.

Adam responded as quickly as he could, while trying to catch his breath, "We've trained for this, but we didn't know what was happening! I looked at my SPG (submersible pressure gauge) and to my surprise, noticed that I was almost out of air."

"We're all right," Kaylee added, "There wasn't enough air in Adam's tank. We had to share our air and *buddy breathe*. It caught us off guard, but it wasn't too difficult." She remembered from her dive certification training that if a diver typically uses 200 psi (pounds per square inch) in five minutes of diving at 45 feet; that was an unusually high air consumption rate. She was using 500 psi, which indicated that something was definately wrong!

Chapter 9

FACE TO FACE WITH THE CAPTAIN

After checking on Adam and Kaylee and seeing they were alright, Luis and two irate parents had their face to face with Steven on deck.

Greg and Dawn shook with fury, exclaiming, "What happened down there?"

Steven admitted he was distracted. "I had a flashback of my childhood when my father died after being thrown overboard in a storm. That is why I was not concentrating on checking the tanks."

Not satisfied, Dawn demanded, "If we're going to continue this treasure hunt, you must reassure us that this kind of lapse in judgment will not happen again!"

The Captain abruptly walked away then turned and said, "Look, I'm sorry that Adam ran out of air at fifty feet. We both should have checked to see if there was enough air in the tank. I'm so glad that Kaylee knew how to buddy breathe. I promise everyone that this won't happen again!" and he slammed his cabin door.

Dawn and Greg were also angry at Adam and Kaylee because they should have known to check their own equipment and not leave it to others prior to any dive.

Adam and Kaylee knew that if they had been able to descend to about 130 feet their time underwater would have been limited. If a SCUBA diver is down deep for a period of time they need to decompress by rising and stopping at different levels. Sometimes it means staying with unwanted company such as 18 foot tiger sharks. Rising to the surface too rapidly is like shaking up a can of soda and then popping off the cap. The gas in the human body also bubbles and causes decompression sickness, or "the bends," not to mention permanent paralysis or even death.

Greg turned his anger on Luis. "The bottom line Luis, is if they hadn't noticed Adam's lack of air, they would have died!"

Luis agreed and followed the Captain to the cabin for an upfront, honest conversation to help gain some lost trust, not only for the Bibas, but for himself as well.

"Steven, *you're driving me up the pole,* and driving me crazy with your constant flashbacks of your father. The memories are giving you more lapses in judgment. I have to tell you, you seem like a *loose cannon,* and are becoming more unpredictable, without regard to others."

"You're right Luis."admitted the captain.

Luis made his way up on deck to where they all caught their breath. The ocean breeze helped to cool them and their tempers.

Luis brought out an old newspaper ad that the captain ran in the past that he had in his personal log book. Luis explained that Steven advertised outside of the Florida area for salvage help because he could not get help from the local divers. The locals thought he was overconfident and took too many risks, like going out to sea in poor conditions.

Luis always felt indebted to Steven and his father for not telling the immigration authorities about his family's escape from Cuba many years ago. He was very grateful to Steven's father for hiring them and allowing him to work for years aboard their salvage ship.

Luis explained about Steven and his dad, "Steven's father told Steven that the severity of the type of hurricane that only happened once every ten years, unearthed treasure from the seafloor. It's the tenth anniversary of his father's death. The Captain's judgment is cloudy, but we want your family to stay with us and we'll all end up rich."

"We're sorry about the death of Steven's father out here," Greg said, "But he can't continue to put anyone's life at risk."

"Safety assurances are definitely important," Luis replied convincingly. "I understand where you're coming from. I will personally guarantee there are no more incidents."

Chapter 10

HIDING BLACK CORAL

Dawn and Greg noticed Kaylee and Adam seemed unusually eager to start diving again after they caught their breath.

"Can we start diving again right now?" Adam asked quickly.

"Yes, if we start our dives again, we may find the rare *black coral*," Kaylee added.

Luis looked at their enraged parents for the okay to start diving again.

"Make sure you remember to have –"

"Our side pouches," Adam said, finishing Luis's sentence.

"Yes ... the fanny packs are for treasures you may find—And remember to check your gauges!" Luis reminded them.

Due to the recent hurricanes in the area, because of the circular wave motion–moving in almost a hula hoop fashion, some of the plants, crabs, sea turtles, oysters, and seahorses that were sitting on the seabed had been unearthed.

Luis added, "This also includes the possibility of having a better chance to find the rare *black coral;* that had broken off the reef and could be found floating with the current, above the seabed, from within the *Bermuda Triangle.* The currents throughout the *Triangle* are affected by the warm Gulf Stream and are continuously turbulent and traveling in a north easterly direction."

Even though the prior dive should have been about 130 feet, and because the Captain did not have enough air in Adam's tank, Kaylee helped him make it to the surface by *buddy breathing.* During their ascent, they were able to see some *black coral* that was drifting with the current.

Without telling anyone they had each stored some in their fanny packs. "Do you think we should tell the Captain that we found the black coral?" Kaylee asked Adam.

"I don't trust Captain Steven," Adam whispered under his breath. "Until he shows that he is going to keep us safe, I'll keep hiding any treasure we find." While looking over his shoulders to check that no one was listening, he added with a grin, "It's like finding Aladdin's magic lamp."

Luis paid special attention to his confident young divers as they prepared for their next dive, noticing they were not leaving their fanny packs, only securely fastening them to their hips.

The cool morning turned into the heat of the day. The plan was to dive before lunch. Greg and Dawn, still hesitant of Steven and Luis's safety check list, not only checked their own gear for their potential 130 foot dive, but made sure to double check Adam and Kaylee's equipment, such as their SPG or submersible pressure gauges.

Greg checked the mechanical gauges known as SPGs that measure the air pressure within the tank. His kids already knew to check their gauges, but Greg did not like to take chances. He reminded them that at the depth they would be diving, they could stay under for a little over an hour, but no more.

Dawn chimed in, "If we don't find anything here at 50 feet, maybe the Captain will let us dive deeper at 130 feet, but only for thirteen minutes."

The plan was to make a dive before lunch, but after double and triple checking all of the dive equipment for safety, Steven gave the okay to wait to dive until after lunch.

In the heat of the afternoon the blue sky held white cotton ball clouds, dotting the bright blue background like polka dots. Everyone on board the old *Acme* salvage vessel, took a lunch break from their tiresome dives for sunken treasure. Their lunch was lobster and crab, dripping in butter, that would absolutely melt in anyone's mouth. Luis brought this recipe from Havana.

Somehow the seagulls could sense lunch was at hand as dozens flew in. Luis explained, "Those are *Laughing Gulls*. They have a maximum wingspan of 4 feet. During these summer months the back and wings of the adult *Laughing Gulls* are dark gray and the bill is dark red." He continued and smiled as he watched the birds, "The gulls are the acrobats of the sky, even with their long legs, they make the seemingly impossible antics appear effortless, catching wind currents with perfect timing and precision while positioning their bodies at just the right angle."

Kaylee and Adam looked through the blinding sun, covering their ears to lesson the strident laughing calls of the gulls.

Adam had been eyeing up the old acoustic guitar near Luis's cot since they had left Dania Beach.

"Luis, I noticed you have a guitar down by your cot. Would you mind if I borrowed it and played some Jimmy Buffet? Maybe that would cover up the gull's screeching cries."

The seagulls were waiting for someone to throw treats of assorted small fish, mussels, clams, or goose-neck barnacles.

"That's a great idea," Luis replied. "We love Jimmy Buffet in these parts."

"It's funny to watch the seagulls dive," Kaylee said smiling. "Like an arrow, straight into the water if they have to. They're bigger than I thought." She added, "Adam, how about playing *Cheeseburger in Paradise*? That's one of my favorites, especially when we hang out at our Stratton Lake cottage back home."

"Yeah, when the wings on those gulls spread out they look like a big kite, floating motionless in mid-air," Adam replied, laughing.

"Luis!" the Captain shouted, "We've got treasure to search for and if we're lucky, *black coral* is waiting, so let's clean up and maybe we can meet up with your pet Seagulls another time."

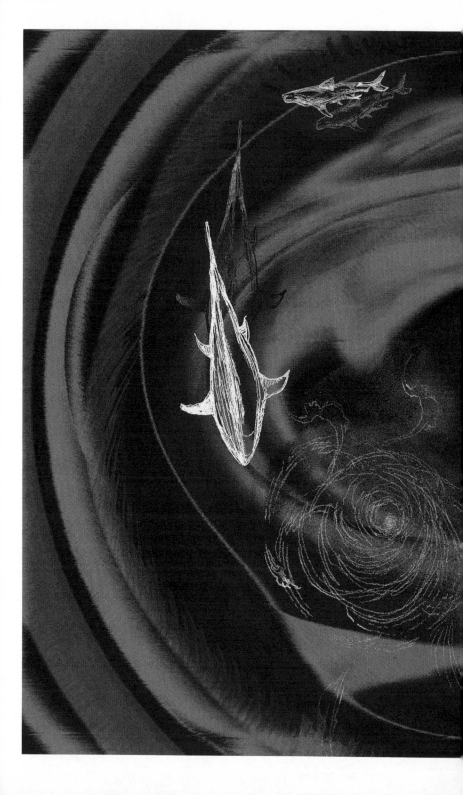

Chapter 11

TENSIONS ARE RISING

Tensions were rising between Greg and Captain Steven. They were about three weeks into their adventure with one week left on their contract to do as many dives as possible. Rather than asking Greg and his family to search for more black coral, the Captain was trying to get everyone except Luis to do more chores on deck. Luis continued to bring up small treasures from the depths of the mysterious triangle, such as, rare silver coins, and a little black coral.

Greg told Dawn, "Earlier in the day, during the first dive of the morning, I saw Luis find a lump of silver coins, a gold bar, and some black coral. I also overheard the Captain tell Luis, 'I know the big payoff of black coral is down there'. I have a feeling those brats, Kaylee and Adam had been finding some and hiding it in their fanny packs."

Captain Steven decided to let Luis go ahead and do more searching inside the Bermuda Triangle, while Adam and Kaylee took a break from mopping the deck, and had their lunch.

Greg looked over at Dawn, as they both nodded in silent agreement, and looked over at their seldom used dive gear, which was just sitting in the corner behind the Captain's rum punch barrel. They put down their deck mops and started putting on their gear. They understood that being deckhands was important but diving and finding treasure was why they came.

After a few minutes of eating Luis's spaghetti, along with the rough seas smashing against the hull of the boat, Kaylee's face turned green and she ran to hang her head over the side of the railing. She got so seasick.

Adam ran over to see if Kaylee was all right and said, while smiling, "The food goes down easy and comes up easy."

Kaylee laughed, and took a big swig of water from

his canteen, "Yeah, and it tasted better going down than coming back up!"

Chapter 12

TOO CLOSE FOR COMFORT

While diving into the *Triangle*, at a depth of 50 feet, Dawn's SPG seemed to be malfunctioning after ten minutes. The dive should have allowed them to stay down at that depth for about 80 minutes, exactly what happened while Kaylee and Adam were diving! Greg and Dawn began their practiced *buddy breathing* technique to slowly make their way to the surface. Dawn was sharing the air from Greg's tank. They both knew there had to be some safety stops to the top, allowing the body to eliminate the excess nitrogen.

In addition to Dawn's SPG issue, they both noticed a large cloud on the water's surface with tiger sharks surrounding it on the other side of the boat. Dawn had seen this type of cloud on previous dive trips. She knew this could have been blood thrown overboard from local fishermen to catch sharks, but she did not see any fishing boats in the area.

Dawn signaled Greg to stay as motionless as possible. Once the frenzy of sharks feeding on the other side of the boat subsided enough they could finish their ascent to the safety of the ship.

"Sharks off the port bow!" Captain Steven yelled. "Where did that floating blood come from?"

Kaylee shouted, while looking at her dive watch, "Mom and Dad should have resurfaced already!"

Adam and Kaylee's tanks were empty which left them helpless to do something for their parents. They could only hold the side of the boat's railing with white knuckles, crying and praying. They just hoped to see bubbles on the water's calm surface to show there was a sign of life below.

Adam was furious and his body was shaking. Kaylee had never seen his face so red.

"Luis get your dive gear on RIGHT NOW! FIND THEM!" Adam demanded.

No one noticed that Greg and Dawn were on the opposite side of the boat waiting for the tiger sharks to dissipate. Luis frantically got his dive gear on as quickly as he ever had, and jumped feet first into the shark infested waters below.

"Wait, Wait!" Adam yelled to Kaylee. The red cloud and the school of sharks magically disappeared as quickly as they became visible.

Captain Steven had to walk away. After about ten minutes, Luis found Greg and Dawn on the opposite side of the boat. All three resurfaced only a few feet away of where the sharks had been feeding. None of them saw any local fishermen throwing blood on the surface of the water baiting sharks to catch. Luis thought to himself that this could be another unexplained *Devil's Triangle* mystery.

This really shook up the Captain. Adam and Kaylee saw Captain Steven go into his cabin, grabbing his bottle of rum punch, which was "hidden" in a barrel. It was typical for Steven and Luis to save and share their rum punch for a nightcap before turning in.

Adam and Kaylee ran over to the side of the boat to meet Greg, Dawn and Luis.

After Luis took off his dive gear, he stormed into the Captain's cabin, demanding some answers. "How could you let this happen, TWICE?"

"We BOTH checked everyone's dive gear!" Steven yelled, as he threw back another large mouthful of rum punch.

Luis replied, "You are lucky no one was hurt. We have to show Greg and Dawn their equipment was perfect for their dive. Hopefully they will understand these mishaps could be added to the list of unexplained mysteries of the *Triangle*."

Chapter 13

THE MOTHER-LOAD

Everyone was exhausted. Steven told Luis to convince Adam to fish for meals so there would be enough food for everyone. Rather than sailing to port for provisions, the Captain lied and told everyone there was enough food and water on board. But he only had rum hidden in his private storage locker.

"Captain, don't you think we are *sailing close to the wind*, or taking too many unnecessary risks?" Luis pleaded.

Steven replied, trying to change the subject, "Hunting for underwater treasure has gone way beyond the x-marks-the-spot style of yesteryear. You know as well as I, new treasure hunting techniques used by some of the larger salvage companies include the use of 3-D map rendering, expensive side-scan sonars, which are usually towed behind a survey boat or mounted on the ship's hull. Also, these survey boats used a "mowing the lawn approach" in which the boat drove over, back and forth, and then moved over 30 feet after each run."

"That's right Captain, I remember. The survey boats also towed 4-ft. long metal fish mounted with side-scan sonar, which is shaped like a torpedo or a big hot dog with fins on the back. This side-scan sonar can help locate piles of ballast rock, which is used to provide stability to a boat or ship. When wreckage is located, the work becomes even more basic: Scuba divers search in grid patterns with metal detectors, scouring the seabed and excavating artifacts by hand."

"Do you remember back in 2001 when scientists used side-scan sonar to survey "Shipwreck Alley?" It is located in the deep waters off the Thunder Bay National Marine Sanctuary and Underwater Preserve in Lake Huron, off the northeast coast of Michigan's lower peninsula. This is the final resting place for scores of ships that had fallen victim to Huron's murky fog banks, sudden gales, and rocky shores. Side-scan sonar permitted explorers to quickly survey and search for downed aircraft and sunken ships."

"Yes, I have heard about Shipwreck Alley. From wooden sailing ships to early steamers to modern vessels, Thunder Bay has taken many ships to their watery graves. More than 100 shipwrecks, dating back to the 1800s, are suspected to rest in the Sanctuary: however, the locations of only 40 are known."

In an era when marine salvage often means remote-control rovers probing deep-water wrecks, Captain Steven reminded Luis, "Over the years we have found bounty from inexpensive strategies developed decades ago."

Luis had tried to convince Captain Steven to consider purchasing some powered air line dive gear rather than scouring the seabed and excavating artifacts by hand.

Captain Steven, in his many years of looking for artifacts buried under the sand or mud, found a few affordable methods that sport divers used to work a site.

Greg and Dawn thought it unusual to see the Captain getting into his dive gear, which he had not done very much during the entire salvage mission. They also overheard him ordering Luis to get his gear on right away.

"When both of you are diving," Greg asked, "Who's driving the boat?"

"The tide" Captain Steven replied.

One such way to find treasure that Luis convinced Steven to try was the use of the vacuum-suction method of salvaging. Steven had been successful in other dive salvage operations in finding treasure because this simply acted like a vacuum cleaner, sucking up the bottom sediment; sand, shells, small rocks, and rare treasure artifacts. It has a discharge tube, which was used to spew debris back into the ocean at the discharge end of the tube and the current carried the fine particles and sand away. Since this vacuum-suction method could be done with two divers it worked perfectly with Luis and Steven. Steven was at the discharge tube, and Luis watched for treasures, such as pieces of eight, precious stones, silver bars, and black coral, that got sucked up by the airlift.

They were so focused on continuing to search for more artifacts that they were not concerned about a few tiger sharks swimming dangerously by.

The use of the hand held fan was Steven's favorite method because it's cheap, easy to make, and can be carried on every dive and without too much effort produces fine results.

Luis used a ping pong paddle as his digger and it could be clipped onto his buoyancy controlled weight belt or carried in his mesh bag. By always digging in the same direction as the current, it usually carried any sediment away, leaving decent visibility in the hole.

When Luis came up on deck for a new tank of air, Kaylee asked, "Can you show us how to use the hand held fan method to find some treasure and then show us how to catalogue it?"

Since there was more success in finding treasure, Luis convinced the Captain to allow the Bibas to contribute more. Bringing up even more valuables would be easy by using the cheap hand held fan method.

No sooner than Luis showed Adam and Kaylee how to find treasure by using the hand held fans, they were bringing up rare coins, silver bars, and gold doubloons. They continued to hide most of the black coral in their fanny packs when no one was looking.

White coral and more black coral had been unearthed off the sea-floor as a result of us using the vacuum-suction method and recent hurricanes. Luis had a hunch that white coral could be of value, and asked Kaylee to gather up any that would float by. She thought gathering white coral was unusual, especially with all the black coral that was within reach.

"After many days of searching, I hope that it's worth it?" Greg questioned. "My legs ache from kneeling on rocky white coral, and they're raw and scratched. Chunks of sand are buried in my scalp and suit, but I can't stop."

The surface of the water was as calm and clear as glass. Greg noticed his reflection and felt his face was several weeks past a five o'clock shadow. Dawn and Kaylee's skin had turned from red to bronze and their hair had bleached whiter from the sun. Adam also had more beard on his face. While still slim and tall, he had added some bulk to his frame from muscling through all the deck chores and swimming against the current during the deepest dives.

When the day of diving ended, everyone made it up on deck for Luis' signature dish of lobster and clams. No one minded when Kaylee and Adam had some rum punch as well.

Greg had forgotten it was his birthday. The Captain and Luis were caught off guard when Dawn, Adam and Kaylee surprised Greg with a simple and different type of birthday celebration. Everyone on board toasted Greg's birthday with a cup of the Captain's rum punch. Rather than wearing store bought party hats, they each made paper old-fashioned Captain's hats out of newspaper that Luis had shown them how to make earlier on the mission. Steven and Luis also gave Greg a birthday present and reached into their private stash of recently discovered treasure and gave him a small piece of black coral.

"It's been a while since I played *Happy Birthday* on the guitar, but here it goes," Adam said with a big grin.

Everyone on board, including Captain Steven joined in singing. It was a very off key version of the world's most popular tune, but Greg enjoyed it very much.

Since the water was tranquil the Bibas decided to go for a quick swim around the boat. Greg and Kaylee were once lifeguards and were accustomed to long swims around Stratton Lake. Dawn could tread water longer than anyone. She once proved to her brother Chuck and a swimming pool full of Army Rangers, that she could hold an army rifle over her head while treading water longer than they could. Adam was a great swimmer as well. Many years ago, Dawn's father Wally had a rule for anyone who wanted to swim the waters of Stratton Lake without an adult being present. When Adam wanted to be at the Biba cottage by himself or with his friends, everyone had to prove they could swim from one side of the lake to the other and back without stopping.

Adam dove in first, with Kaylee following, and then Dawn and Greg. One after the other dove in off the bow with Adam splashing everyone, as they made their leisurely swim in the cool and presently calm water. They all followed the leader slowly back up the ACME dive ladder. It felt great for the Bibas to relax and feel no pressure to bring up black coral or any other treasures.

Dawn was fortunate to have been on many trips as a dive coordinator in the waters off the Florida coast when she was in college. One of the favorite parts of her experiences was seeing all of the different types of marine life. This salvage mission for treasure reminded her of when she saw sharks, rays, eels, dolphins, barracuda, puffer fish, waterspouts, and different colors of coral.

Luis had been on many salvage missions with Captain Steven over the years and on a few treasure hunting tourist trips. He wrote of how the personalities of people on board, both young and old can change so quickly while out in the *Triangle*.

In Luis' private travel log he documented:

LUIS' PERSONAL LOG
July 22 (Greg's B-day) Day 27

We have been in the Triangle *now longer at one time than I have ever experienced before with treasure hunting tourists.*

I've seen many changes: Are they coincidental, Or from the mysterious superstitions of being in the Triangle?

Everyone's personality on board changes almost daily ... Is it the fact that we are having some success with finding treasure that is making everyone more greedy? Is it the fact that being in the Triangle has changed everyone's personality? I've seen Steven's personality change from friend to task master ... Is it the Captain's greed of successfully finding black coral, or personal pride to have a successful salvage mission, on this 10th Anniversary of his father's death at sea? Adam and Kaylee's carefree attitudes have changed also. After a little time at sea Adam and Kaylee were having an awesome time and learning how to find some trinkets in the sand. I believe spending more time inside the Triangle has somehow changed their carefree attitudes. This has made finding treasure more of an obsession. I have not seen them find any black coral yet, but I do believe Adam and Kaylee might be hiding some for themselves.

As far as my observations of Greg and Dawn, they are doing the best they can to be successful treasure hunters, but I can tell they are at the breaking point at times with the Captain's carelessness. Even though we are scheduled to be out here in the Bermuda Triangle for a few more days, I feel that we have more unusual experiences in store for us.

Chapter 14

PIRATES

It is always advisable to contact the Bermuda Maritime Operations Center (formerly Bermuda Harbor Radio) before you start your voyage for Bermuda and provide information related to your vessel, crew, and equipment. This will allow them to track your course and guide you as necessary.

Everyone was allowed to sleep in a little as a treat from the Captain for all the treasure salvaged yesterday.

"Dawn, do you think the Captain or Luis connected with the coast guard prior to our sailing adventure?" Greg asked. "I hope they were provided the necessary information of our boat and crew."

"The waves are calm for now; *plain sailing*. Smooth and easy progress is being made." Luis had a hunch that a severe storm was coming, because of the red skies that appeared this morning.

Adam and Kaylee started their back breaking chores of mopping the deck. When lucky enough to catch fish, they were asked to clean those for all on board.

"Hey Adam, do you see that small boat out there that's been sitting on the horizon?" Kaylee questioned curiously. She pulled out her sketchbook for a quick drawing of the boat getting closer.

"Yeah, they have been there for a while, but I noticed they're coming closer to us."

The Captain and Luis knew the strategy of pirates is to wait in the distance and then come in for a quick score. The scavengers would assume that if a salvage boat stayed in an area for an extended period of time, there must be some successful treasure hunting and gathering happening. The pirates would use their smaller, quicker boat to gain on any research vessel that would try to get away.

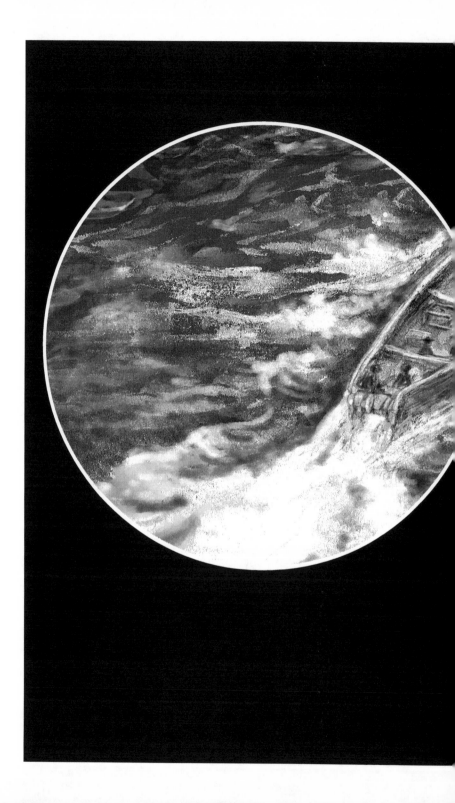

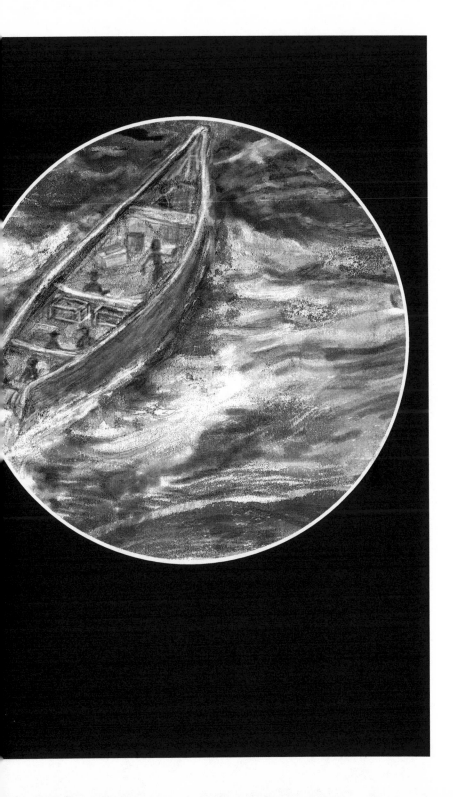

Luis used his binoculars, watching the small boat approach off the starboard bow. The small boat was coming in at a fast speed, with enough sea spray coming off the bow to get all on board soaked.

"Kaylee, put down your sketchbook and quickly grab that big bag of white coral that I asked you to gather," Luis ordered.

The Captain knew if this was a boat full of pirates and he tried to start this salvage boat to get away, everyone's life would be in danger.

When the Captain was much younger there were more pirates in these coastal waters. Since there were fewer Coast Guard ships on patrol, the fishermen and treasure hunters would have to find creative ways to slow the marauders down as they tried to board any vessels.

Steven quickly told everyone, "Stay calm, do everything that I say, and we may make it out of here alive. Grab fishing poles or pretend you're doing deck chores."

When the group of men slowly approached, the Captain, Luis, Adam and Greg hauled their trunks of gold coins, silver bars, and black coral, down below deck. Steven's plan was to keep all valuables away from anyone that could see them when they boarded.

To Adam's surprise, he saw Luis and Steven take the seat cushions off the benches that his family had used so many times during their adventure. They lifted the secret lids and placed their treasure trove into the bottom of the seats, then covered everything with rope, fishing nets, and tackle. He also noticed the Captain grabbed a small hand-gun from the bench and put it in his pants pocket.

Steven quickly whispered, "With my experiences dealing with pirates taking over boats, I've never seen it happen, but if you upset them too much, it's been told that they will not think twice about throwing everyone overboard to the sharks."

If these were indeed pirates coming aboard, Luis knew the first place to look for valuables would be the Captain's quarters.

Our new "friends" pulled alongside our boat and expected to be allowed to tie on. It wasn't until one of the pirates finally asked for a ladder to climb up, that Dawn, who was stalling for time, yelled over to them, "I'll be there in a moment. I've hooked onto a big one."

After about a minute, Dawn made her way over to the pirates boat with the ladder.

As each man made their way up the ladder, Dawn's eyes got as big as pie plates when she saw each man's similar tattoo of a skull and crossbones

Two of the men seemed friendly and outgoing, asking for water. Dawn and Kaylee could tell one man was looking around rather suspiciously, not saying a word. Dawn tried to be creative and stall for time while the guys were hiding their treasure down below. One man wore a red and white striped shirt, while the other two had ripped cut off shorts and needed shoes.

"So, are you two ladies having any luck fishing? It's rather unusual to have women out here with no men on board."

The most quiet, uninvited guest made his way past the Captain's rum punch barrel, took a tin cup full, while wiping his sleeve for the extra punch that missed his mouth.

"I'm going to try to *stem the tide* as we quickly head up on deck. Hopefully, I can prevent a situation from becoming worse than it already is," Luis whispered.

He started to go below deck when Steven, Luis and Greg made their way up noticing a tense situation.

"Welcome friends," Steven said, as he felt the handgun in his pants pocket.

Casually, Luis invited everyone over to a section of the boat, far away from the black coral, gold coins, and silver bars below.

"I can see by the *cut of your jib* that you men could use some fresh clothes to wear and a shave. We can help you out with that," Luis mentioned casually, while smiling, to try to lighten the tense situation that was unfolding.
"We're not going to *make waves* here," Luis added, as they strolled over to the bow. "We don't want to cause any trouble."

"Kaylee, our friends look thirsty and hungry. Can you please bring over some fresh water and lobster," Captain

Steven politely asked.

"I'm Captain Teach, great-great-great-grandson of Edward Teach "Blackbeard." It looks like you have been in this location for a couple days," he said gruffly as he adjusted the eye patch over his left eye.

"We've had some luck catching some fish and lobster," Steven tried to say convincingly.

"How about you and your crew?" Steven asked. "Have you had any luck fishing recently?"

After what seemed like an eternity, Captain Teach finally asked, "What do you have below deck?"

After hearing this from below, Adam looked around and grabbed a harpoon off the wall. He was not going to let pirates take what their family had painstakingly searched for.

"What's that in the dive bags by your feet little girl?" Captain Teach asked firmly.

"It's just some white coral and trinkets that we picked up while we were out here fishing," Kaylee tried to reply convincingly.

Captain Teach did not believe her at all, thinking there would at least be some gold, silver bars, and black coral.

Just as the pirates were getting tired of the conversations, Captain Teach grabbed the bag of white coral by Kaylee's feet and started to head down below deck.

Dawn knew her husband would try to stop the pirates before they made their way to their defenseless son, even if it meant him getting hurt. Adam squeezed the handle of the harpoon, ready to fire if needed. Luckily, at that moment, a Coast Guard ship that was passing by about 50 yards away, noticed two boats tied up together. They had heard rumors of pirates in the area.

While heading down below deck the pirates did not see the Coast Guard ship or everyone on deck, waving their arms and pointing down below.

Adam's hands were shaking as he saw the shadow of footsteps starting to come down the stairs.

"This is the Coast Guard, you are not authorized to be in this area, you are ordered to come out with your hands up!"

"My son is down below, please hurry and help him," Dawn pleaded.

The pirates heard the orders of the Coast Guard and came up with their hands up, with one man still holding the bag of useless white coral over his head.

It looked as though Pirate Teach had been through this before. The pirates put their hands behind their backs, waiting to be cuffed. Laughing, Captain Teach only responded, "You got lucky this time, we'll be back."

They were still in shock, feeling as if they were going to be killed by the pirates.

The Coast Guard knew Captain Steven from so many years of them sharing the coastal waters. As he escorted the officers and the pirates off the boat, they overheard him saying they were all fine and having luck with our fishing. Since they did not seem too concerned about Steven's mental well-being, and our being relieved about the pirates being taken into custody, it made us relax some more.

The Captain's split personality showed more after the Coast Guard was out of sight. Then no one was surprised when the only thing Steven had to say was, "From now on, whatever we find goes into the vessel's treasure chest below. If there are more pirates in the area, at least if we get boarded they will have a hard time finding anything of value."

Luis had to respond to the Captain, "Is this one way to *show your true colors* or show who you really are?"

Everyone was shocked to see Adam, as he came up from below deck, shaking, and still gripping the handle of the harpoon he had grabbed off the wall.

Luis quietly stepped toward Adam and whispered, "Adam, why don't we take that harpoon and see if we can get a nice big tuna."

Luis then stepped to the side of the deadly harpoon and gently guided the arrow towards the deck floor.

Watching the Coast Guard take the pirates away made everyone, including Adam, relax.

Steven went over to his rum punch barrel and got everyone on board a tin cup full.

"*Bottoms Up,*" Luis suggested as he encouraged all to relax and take a drink.

Luis quickly borrowed his guitar back from Adam and played some more Jimmy Buffet songs. He hoped this could take their minds off the close call with the pirates.

"Here's a couple of my favorites," Luis suggested. "I hope you'll like *Havana Daydreamin',* and *Margaritaville.*"

We all admired Luis's guitar playing. His smooth playing along with a few more tin cups of rum punch made everyone feel a bit more relaxed.

Chapter 15

THE STORM

Red sky at night, sailor's delight. Red sky in morning, sailors take warning, was a rhyme used as a rule of thumb for weather forecasting during the past two millennia. It is based on the reddish glow of the morning or evening sky, caused by haze or clouds related to storms in the region. The saying assumes that more such clouds are coming in from the west.

The skies were red this morning, and the warm waters were perfect for a tropical storm. Over the years Luis and Captain Steven had been through many storms at sea. They had been lucky enough to avoid hurricanes if there was a chance to sail around them.

To convince the Captain to take more precautions Luis even read from his book of nautical meteorological wind force terms and descriptions used by mariners for hundreds of years. "Water from the surface of the ocean evaporates because of the high temperatures. Hot air rises, cool air sinks. As the hot air is rising, surrounding warm moist air flows in, and since the earth is rotating, air spirals toward the center rather than traveling in a straight line. Captain, there are more hazy clouds coming in from the west. I think we should take precautions for everyone's safety and not do any diving today."

Luis knew the Captain's greed was so intense that he wouldn't listen to any warning signs. He felt he had to add one more observation, hoping we could take more storm related precautions and not dive today.

"Captain, this storm is brewing up to be like Tropical Storm Brenda of 5 years ago. We were lucky enough to barely miss by sailing around the worst part. Don't you remember a small tornado or waterspout spawned by the storm damaged a commercial airliner and was apparently responsible for winds of 92 mph?"

"Let me worry about the weather forecasts!" Steven sternly replied. "Don't be silly. You know I don't believe in any of those *Triangle* mystery stories."

The Captain did have the vessel's radar on, but being in the middle of the Bermuda Triangle, the electromagnetic interference or distortion caused the radar to not accurately show the oncoming storm.

Greg and Dawn were trying to figure out a way to get the word to a passing ship or another coast guard vessel of their situation. They figured Luis would assume command because Steven's mental state was in question.

The feeling of déjà vu was undeniable. Being held hostage on this salvage boat was similar to when they were held at gunpoint by the Israeli secret service on their last adventure. The only difference was that the agents guarding the son of the Prime Minister of Israel at the Stratton Lake Jewish Camp did not know who they we were.

Recalling instances of Steven's irrationality was easy when they thought back to how he convinced them to change their dive plans. He actually admitted he could be distracted on dives because of the 10th anniversary of his father's death on a *Bermuda Triangle* salvage mission. Another instance of the Captain's sanity being at question was when he lied about having enough food and water on board hidden in his private locker.

In addition, Greg and Dawn felt Captain Steven's dual personality showed after the Coast Guard arrested the pirates. The only thing he did was turn around and tell them that whatever treasure they found from now on went to the vessel's treasure chest.

They tried to use the radio to signal mayday, but there was nothing but static. Their laptops were also useless. Greg whispered, "I'll bet nothing is working because we're in the *Triangle.*"

Chapter 16

THE LAST DIVE

With only time for one more dive, and not finding as much black coral treasure as before, Captain Steven ordered Luis to sail deeper into the *Triangle*. He told all aboard that since this was the deepest diving of the trip; about 197 feet, or a height of a twenty story building, they were all going to use scuba tanks filled with the mixture of air called "Tri-mix". The Tri-mix requires additional gear and training; neither of which Greg and his family had.

The Captain did warn everyone to be careful of possible explosions that could occur.

Greg did not like the smile that came on the Captain's face when he added, "We all need to be careful because the air itself becomes toxic as we go beyond 184 ft."

Steven continued and read parts of his old U.S. Navy Diving Manual and short articles relating to oxygen toxicity. "During filling, there is a risk of fire due to the use of oxygen and a risk of explosion due to the use of high pressure gases. The concentration of unreactive gases, such as nitrogen and helium are planned and checked to avoid nitrogen narcosis and decompression sickness." The Captain added, "The percent of gas components vary depending on the dive. The deeper one goes, the less there will be oxygen and nitrogen and the more there will be helium. Air, which was first used in diving tanks, contains roughly 20% oxygen, and 80% nitrogen."

Luis was happy that he did warn everyone regarding the addition of helium to the nitrogen/oxygen combo, rather than using the safer Nitrox Mixture, and was for a growing number of advanced divers only. Helium is definitely not for the "once in a while" diver, and is used for respiration in deep water instead of nitrogen.

Hearing this, Dawn quickly ran down into her cabin and pulled out the laptop to try more research about the potential safety concerns of diving too deep, but her efforts were in vain. She did notice a pipe that was starting to leak in the engine room and quickly told the Captain.

"I'll get that leak stopped as quickly as possible," Steven replied half heartedly.

She recalled that in her many dive experiences, the trouble with nitrogen in this situation is that it is a fairly heavy gas, and is soluble in blood at high pressure. Dawn also remembered that nitrogen narcosis can cause a strange sense of euphoria, like being drunk, and makes the diver unable to assess dangers. Just as working drunk on the surface is not a good idea, working drunk at the bottom of the sea can be extremely hazardous.

Adam and Kaylee had been painstakingly doing their boring deck chores and were exhausted. In between the mopping and cleaning fish Adam asked Kaylee, "So what are you going to do with your part of the treasure?"

While smiling, "I don't know, maybe use it for part of another adventure someday?"

While meeting Greg back on deck, Dawn concluded, "Diving too deep would mean having nitrogen dissolved into our blood, and we would have to remember to decompress (on surface) very slowly, to allow nitrogen to come back out of the blood to be breathed out. If we come up too quickly we'd have a huge risk of the nitrogen being released from the blood too quickly and forming bubbles in our bloodstreams."

Greg added, "Yes, this can cause blockages. The condition is called the *Bends,* is very painful, and life threatening." He added, "One way to avoid all these problems is to avoid nitrogen. Divers who stay down for long periods use a mixture of 20% Oxygen and 80% Helium."

Overhearing this, Luis chimed in trying to calm everyone's nerves by saying, "Helium is used for a number of reasons – It is light, cheap, and does not dissolve in blood the same way that nitrogen does. It cannot be toxic to the diver or corrosive to equipment. It's well known that helium is proving its worth as a safe and reliable mix."

Dawn's additional dive experience showed Hydrogen has been used in deep diving as mixes but is very explosive when mixed with more than about 4% to 5% oxygen (such as oxygen found in breathing gas).

While smiling, she added, "Like helium, it makes your voice sound higher if you suck it in. The hydrogen - oxygen mix when used as a diving gas is sometimes referred to as *Hydrox.*"

Captain Steven knew that Hydrogen had a very broad flammability range and that keeping air or oxygen from mixing with hydrogen inside confined spaces is very important. Even small amounts of liquid hydrogen can be explosive with air, and only a small amount of energy is required to ignite it.

Luis reminded Steven under his breath, "An uncontrolled release of a flammable gas like hydrogen may lead to a fire or explosion, particularly in a confined area where potential ignition sources are present like boilers or hot surfaces."

Common sense told Greg and Dawn that flammable liquids can spread a fire across a workplace floor and allow flames to come into contact with gas cylinders.

While pointing to a Warning Sticker on the side of the dive tanks, Greg butted in, "After all that you've put my family through, I'm not surprised you didn't tell us earlier you had tanks aboard that could explode."

The crew was under Captain's orders to gather as much black coral as possible and to dive deeper.

He reminded everyone, "Do this last dive and I know we will all be rich."

They quickly jumped into the unusually warm water. Getting below the surface was difficult. The waves were so rough because of the storm that was brewing. The waves under the surface were being forced into a circular motion. This great turmoil under the surface unearthed more black coral. Quickly gathering this *floating treasure* was much easier than at any other point of their dive trip.

Now that the Bibas were under water, Captain Schultz ordered Luis, "Go and grab my neoprene dive suit and some large hose clamps. We need to cut a patch from the suit to fit over the hole in the pipe, and see that it holds over the leak in the engine room."

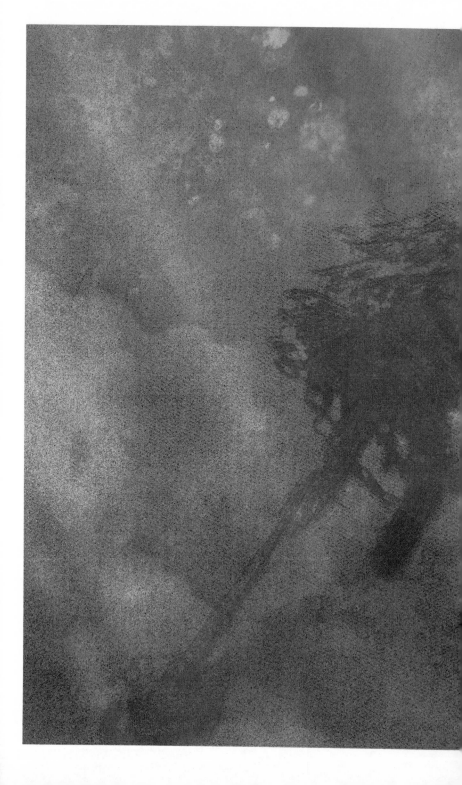

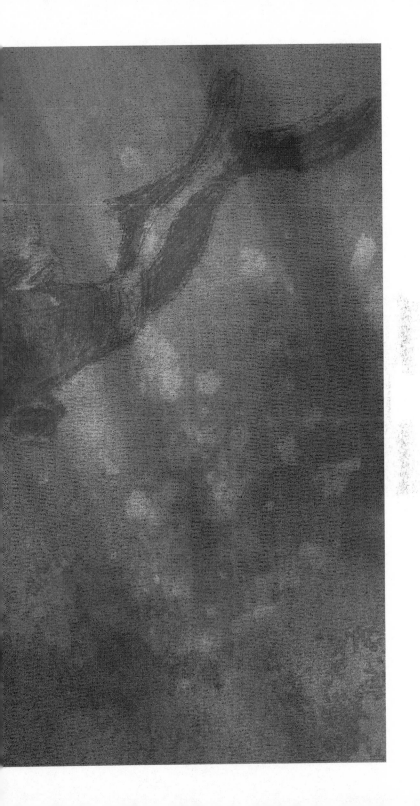

The original plan on this last descent was to dive deeper, but since the black coral was floating much higher and the fact that a severe storm was coming, diving at 50 feet was a relief. Greg motioned to everyone with a point to his dive watch that they were running out of time. He then pointed to the surface so they could all make their slow ascent to the surface. This ascent to the surface included, resting for two minutes, then going to 40 feet for one minute, 30 feet for one minute, 20 feet for two minutes, then 15 feet for two to five minutes. Finally, creeping our way up and maybe stopping at 5 to 10 feet for 30 seconds to a minute. This added together would compare to ascending roughly 12 floors in a building.

By the time they resurfaced the boat was tossing and turning like someone having a bad dream. The shoreline was in sight and white-caps were starting to top at giant or rogue wave sizes, which were steep and tall walls of water.

The Captain and Luis both knew that each wave would reach 30 feet tall, occasionally they could coincide at the right moment and create the "Freak" wave that can be over 100 feet. They also knew without a doubt, this area is prone to rogue waves, and is possible anywhere you get multiple storms together.

They made their way across the surface of the water, battling waves that were hitting the sides of their heads, like being in the center of the ring, being pounded by a heavyweight boxing champion.

Steven quickly ordered Luis to take the helm. He yelled, "Small vessels can get swamped by these waves, but sometimes we can ride the wave if they hit the bow straight on."

Luis thought this tropical storm was producing force winds at approximately sixty five mph.

"We're in deep water now, and deep trouble!"

Captain Steven was so concerned about collecting black coral from the last dive, and sealing the pipe that was leaking down in the hold, that the extra tanks containing the Tri-mix, which also contained helium, were being thrown around the deck like rag dolls because he forgot to secure them properly.

Chapter 17

THE EXPLOSION

Captain Steven ordered Luis to start the pumps because they were taking on too much water from the powerful storm, as well as the leaking pipe in the engine room.

"We didn't get the pumps serviced properly before we left on the salvage mission. The stress on the motor is starting to make the pumps overheat. We should either use them sparingly or we might have to abandon ship," Luis tried to plead.

"You keep those pumps running. Never mind the smoke from the pumps. We need to keep the water off this boat. I will take full responsibility."

"Captain, we may start a fire!" Luis yelled one more time.

The tropical storm winds were now topping at full strength of seventy miles per hour.

Greg, Dawn, Adam and Kaylee were bouncing with the waves wondering if they should try to make it to the boat, which was about fifty yards away, or try to swim to the dangerous rocky shoreline. This island was located within the Turks and Caicos region. In Greg's lifeguard training he remembered swimming to the shore would mean swimming around the rip current that was taking the water away from shore. This was an area of about 50 feet wide where the water appeared lower and whitecaps were less prominent.

"Where are you going Adam?" Dawn yelled above the storm.

Without hesitation, Kaylee's lifeguard instincts kicked in and she tried to catch up to him.

Steven and Luis were so busy with saving the salvage vessel, they didn't see Kaylee help Adam climb up the dive ladder. He quickly took off his fins and handed them to

Kaylee as she waited at the bottom of the ladder. He quietly set his weight belt on deck, but left his tank on his back.

"What are you going to get Adam?"

"You'll see soon enough. I'll be right back. I think the boat's going to explode."

The pump was sparking and red hot. "Captain, we better *batten down the hatches!"* Luis demanded. We have to prepare the ship by covering or securing what we can."

By this time Adam had snuck his way back to his cabin for his dive knife and the Captain's quarters for a flare gun.

"Grab that dive tank Luis, before it's thrown down into the hot pump!" the Captain yelled to Luis.

Adam and Kaylee had gotten far enough away by now to avoid being seen and were getting closer to Greg and Dawn. Adam had cut his leg on some sharp rocks sticking out of the water and was falling behind Kaylee. She made her way back to him, trying to avoid the whitecaps by swimming under the water. Kaylee quickly thought to herself this is going to be nothing like my lifeguarding saves at the South Park Beach. This is going to be the biggest rescue of my life. Performing a rescue in these types of conditions was difficult even for Kaylee. By turning him around while she was under water and then being able to grab his chest, she was able to swim the sidestroke so he could save his energy.

At that moment a very large, 55 foot, unexpected, and very dangerous, Rogue Wave came out of nowhere and ripped apart the back deck. The whole stern looked like a bathtub.

The dive tank that Luis tried to reach was thrown down into the pump when another huge wave hit the bow.

As Luis stated earlier, with the dive tank now being free to release flammable gas, it hit the hot surface of the pump as it was sparking.

Steven and Luis had no choice but to evacuate the Acme Salvage Vessel, with only a life raft to save them.

"*Abandon Ship,* watch out Captain, she's gonna BLOW!"

Chapter 18

THE RESCUE

Greg and Dawn woke up next to each other, on a small stretch of sand about the size of the end zone of a football field. They were hearing the loud sound of the Coast Guard's Search and Rescue helicopter; a Twin Engine Sikorski Jayhawk MH-60T. Kaylee was standing up on a set of large rocks a short distance away, waving her arms and pointing to large SOS rocks that they placed in the sand next to them in the middle of the night. There was no place for the chopper to land on the narrow rocky island.

Large gashes that needed medical attention were on Greg's arm and Dawn and Adam's legs. The gashes were from the sharp rocks they passed as they made it to the safety of the beach. They slowly sat up, spitting out sand and salt water they had swallowed, after they made their harrowing escape and swam from the boat's explosion last night.

Looking through the blinding sun, they observed a man jumping from the side of the chopper, feet first, and holding his mask in place because of the 20 foot drop to the white caps below.

"How far did we swim last night after the ship blew up?" Greg asked, rubbing the back of his neck which was still sore.

Shrugging her shoulders, Dawn remarked, "About fifty yards. We all knew to swim with the current to avoid getting sucked under," Dawn replied. "I guess we got lucky avoiding the sharks and the jagged rocks only a few feet below. It looks like our rescue hero is swimming like a fish toward us, rather than swimming to Captain Steven and Luis."

Captain Steven and first mate Luis were floating helplessly off the jagged coastline with no paddles in their sinking life raft. They were waving their arms, for what Greg and Dawn would call some selfish attention from above.

Luis noticed fins rising onto the surface a few yards away. This could have been a "great white." The unwelcome sight of sharks brought back memories from when he was a child. He remembered waiting for his family to be rescued by Steven and their salvage company. Times were much harder for Luis when he was younger. The family's homemade raft was made to escape the hardships of Havana, not the hungry sharks. But, hungry man-eaters typically frequented these waters and were making their presence known, easily smelling blood floating around their sinking raft, creeping ever so close.

"We've got to try to stop that leak in the side of the life raft!" Luis shouted. "Captain, we are *caught between the devil and the deep blue sea.* What are we going to do to get out of this dangerous predicament?"

At that point, another Coast Guard Police Department Officer, who was also an ex-navy seal, jumped into the shark infested waters, making sure Steven and Luis were each raised by a basket to the warmth and security of the chopper's interior.

After the rescue swimmer attended to the cuts on Greg's arm and Dawn and Adam's legs, he quickly swam back to the helicopter and was also raised up by basket.

Greg and Dawn watched the Sikorsky Jayhawk fly off towards the safety of the Florida coast.

"Well, they were *like rats deserting a sinking ship,*" Greg commented while smiling.

"Where did you learn that and what does that mean?"

"It was one of the sayings that Luis had told me and it is a way of saying that people have to leave or abandon an activity or organization."

It seemed as though Kaylee was alright, considering all the work put into the SOS rescue throughout the evening.

Greg told Dawn, Adam and Kaylee, "The rescue swimmer that helped bandage our cuts and bruises, told me a coast guard ship would be notified and would be coming back for us as soon as possible. We should be all right until then, because the Coast Guard left us some blankets, food and water."

Dawn sighed, "Thank God we're alive! It's too bad that after all the diving for gold doubloons, silver bars, the rare black coral, and all the close calls we had over the last month, the only satisfaction we have is to see Captain Steven and Luis taken away by the Coast Guard."

Kaylee slid off the razor sharp rocks where she was resting, cautiously moving, but still tearing her dive suit. Luckily she had only minor scrapes.

Kaylee said, "We couldn't help but overhear what you said mom. The only satisfaction was to see Captain Steven and Luis taken away, and there was no treasure."

Dawn questioned Greg, "What happened to our share of the treasure that Steven took from us before the ship exploded?"

"I saw him throw a backpack into the bottom of the life raft before Luis lowered it into the water."

"How did the Coast Guard helicopter get here so soon?" Dawn asked.

Adam added, "Before the explosion, I ran into my cabin and grabbed my dive knife and reached for the flare gun on the Captain's desk, guessing we would need them."

"Thank goodness Adam had the good sense to fire the orange colored rescue gun into the sky before he and I left the other side of the boat. Just as we cleared the boat a passing plane or ship must have seen the flare shot in the sky and called the distress signal into the Coast Guard," Kaylee explained.

When the boat exploded, some of the masts fell into the waters nearby. Fortunately, Kaylee and Adam held onto it. During the commotion, when Steven and Luis weren't looking and the life raft drifted by, they were extremely quiet and able to get close enough to try to hold on to the side of the yellow raft. Steven pushed them and the ship's mast away.

"I drove my dive knife into the side of it, just low enough so it couldn't be plugged, before we let loose of the raft," Adam confessed.

"That doesn't look like your yellow backpack, Kaylee?" Greg questioned.

"While you, Adam, and Mom were being attended to by the Coast Guard rescuer, I noticed something red floating along the rocks below us. I made my way down. It was the Captain's red backpack," Kaylee said laughing. "It must have fallen out of the big life raft as it was sinking."

"Yeah, and if you look inside, there's probably a couple half empty bottles of the Captain's favorite rum punch that helped to make the backpack more buoyant. Kaylee was struggling to lift the backpack, so I helped her bring it up to the rocks so we could take a look inside," Adam said with a huge grin.

"Well, show us what's inside!" Dawn shouted.

To everyone's astonishment, there were gold doubloons and silver bars in the backpack, as well as a couple empty bottles of the Captain's favorite rum punch, all painstakingly salvaged and brought aboard. Also included was much of the rare black coral that had been missing recently from the boat's treasure chest.

The Coast Guard rescue ship returned soon with a team of investigators to document what happened and to salvage anything of significance or value before it sank.

Greg, Dawn, and the kids were transferred to the Coast Guard ship for medical treatment.

After a few weeks of recovery at home, Adam got a phone call from a friend that he had stayed in touch with since he lived in Peru several years earlier. His friend, Juan Carlos was a mountain guide in northern Peru. Juan asked him if he would be interested in coming back to Peru to help resolve the rumors about new treasures being discovered within the walls of Peru's famed Machu Picchu Citadel.

Kaylee and Adam looked at each other and nodded in agreement with what to say to their parents if they ever had the chance to go on another exciting adventure.

Adam started by asking Mom and Dad, "Do you remember when Kaylee and I lived and studied in South America years ago? One of the things I studied was the archaeology of Peru and Kaylee reminded us that she obtained her degree in Chilean and Peruvian history."

"Since we both became fluent in Spanish and met people in our fields that we trust, why don't we take some of the money we'll get in exchange for this *black coral treasure hunt* and take a vacation to Peru?" Kaylee suggested.

"Why Peru?" Greg asked Adam.

"We have made contacts who are guides in the area, that say it could be the most important archaeological find ever unearthed within the walls of Machu Picchu Citadel. In a worldwide internet poll in 2007, the Citadel was also voted as one of the newest Seven Wonders of the World." Adam added, "We could search for the tomb of Pachacuti Inca Yupanqui, the Inca ruler, built in 1450. We could find gold, silver and precious metals, making it the largest discovery at the famed site."

"COUNT US IN! When can we go?" Dawn shouted.

"Here we go again — another adventure!" Greg said with a grin.

ABOUT THE AUTHOR

Greg Biba has lived in central Wisconsin most of his life, and enjoyed the sights, sounds and mysteries that come from the lakes in the area. He currently lives in Waupaca, Wisconsin with his wife and their son and daughter.

Being certified scuba divers, Greg and his family have enjoyed diving in parts of the Great Lakes and all over Wisconsin.

ADVENTURE I
A Stratton Lake Mystery
Kidnapping, Gangsters, Escape, and Treasure

Also, a long time band director, Greg has published

Quick Fix
Band Instrument Repair Manual
GIA Publishing, Chicago, Illinois

Made in the USA
Columbia, SC
25 September 2020